LET the DICE DECIDE

Illustrated by Sophie Foster

Edited by Jonny Marx
Cover design by John Bigwood
Designed by Derrian Bradder

Buster Books

INTRODUCTION

Let the dice decide what you doodle, draw, colour and write in this book. There are creatures to create, monsters to mash up, names to randomize, superheroes to assemble, adventures to plot, futures to predict and much more.

HERE'S WHAT YOU DO ...

To complete a mash-up, all you do is roll your dice. The first number you get shows you what part of a drawing or word you need to draw or write to start with. Roll again and again to add more elements to your mash-up. For example, if you were making a monster on pages 4 and 5, and you rolled a 2, a 5 and a 4, the parts of the picture you'd need to put together are shown here:

SHAPE   PATTERN   HAIRSTYLE

And here's the monster you
would make. Handsome, isn't it?

Did you know
one dice is also
called a die?

Why not use sheets of paper to create different
combinations and to challenge your friends to see
who can come up with the craziest concoction?

There are cut-out dice at the back of the
book. You can fold and glue these or use
plastic dice if you have some to hand.

WHAT ARE YOU WAITING FOR?

Ready? Steady ... ROLL!

The monster mash

What shape will it be?

Which pattern?

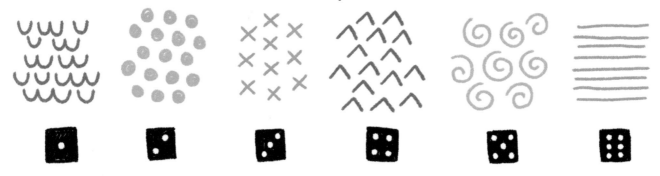

Which hairstyle will it have?

Draw your monster in the frame.

The NAME generator

First Name

Klaus   Debbie   Inferno   Spike   Carrie   Kevin

Middle Name

 or or 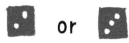   or or

The   Von

Surname

Destroyer   Poop   Terrible   Stink   Hairy   Spotty

This menacing monster is called:

....

CREATE A CHARACTER

Which hairstyle?

Which eyes?

Which nose?

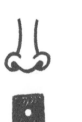    

Which mouth?

Draw the features on the character above.

SHADE IN SOME SUPERHEROES

What colour are their tops and leggings? Roll once for each character.

Give each superhero an emblem or crest.
Draw it in the empty space on each costume.

What colour are their boots and pants? Roll once for each character.

What colour are their capes? Roll once for each character.

NAME YOUR SUPERHEROES

Roll once for each first name.

Starfox Galactic Captain Professor Power Mega

Roll once for each surname.

Oxide Pluto Obscure Weewee Phantom Flame

What powers will they possess?

The ability to freeze things

The ability to stop hiccups

The ability to set fire to things

The ability to stop time

The ability to run fast

The ability to burp on command

GREETINGS!
MY NAME IS

....

SUPER POWER:

....

....

HELLO!
MY NAME IS

....

SUPER POWER:

....

....

Robot-O-Matic

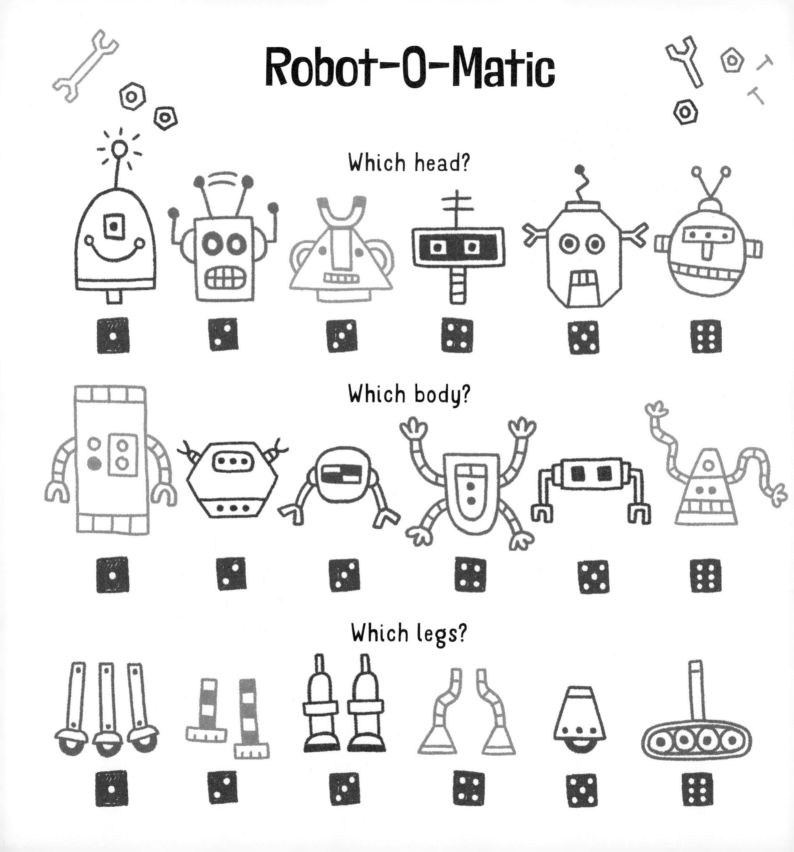

Which head?

Which body?

Which legs?

Draw your radical robot in the frame.

THE SHORT-STORY FACTORY:

Fairytale Fiasco

	NOUNS	ADJECTIVES	VERBS	RANDOM	
⚀	PRINCESS	GOOD-LOOKING	BURPS	CHICKENS	⚀
⚁	GOBLIN	WICKED	SNEEZES	SHEEP	⚁
⚂	WOLF	LONELY	DANCES	CHILDREN	⚂
⚃	OLD LADY	CREEPY	SLEEPS	FLOWERS	⚃
⚄	DRAGON	STRANGE	SCREAMS	BRICKS	⚄
⚅	WITCH	KIND	SPITS	BOOKS	⚅

Roll a dice to complete the story on the opposite page. Each time you reach a dotted line, roll to select a random word from the column with the matching symbol.

Do not use the same word twice – roll until you get a new word.

Once upon a time, a ☆☆☆☆☆☆☆☆☆☆☆☆☆☆☆☆☆☆☆☆☆☆☆☆☆ ◎◎◎◎◎◎◎◎◎◎◎◎◎◎◎◎◎◎◎ lived in a little wooden hut in the forest. She was living a peaceful life until a ☆☆☆☆☆☆☆☆☆☆☆☆☆☆☆☆☆☆☆☆☆ ◎◎◎◎◎◎◎◎◎◎◎◎◎◎◎◎ knocked on her door and said, "Help! Help! An ogre is in my house and I need to get rid of it before it ▦▦▦▦▦▦▦▦▦▦▦▦▦▦▦▦▦ in every room!" Without further ado, they ran to the house and found that the ogre had eaten all of the .... and the ....! The ogre's footprints disappeared into the woods, but no one dared follow them.

The End

DRAW-A-SAURUS

What shape will it be?

Will it have horns on its head or spines on its back?

Which pattern will it have?

DRAW YOUR DINOSAUR IN THE FRAME.

NAME-A-SAURUS

Prefix

Tyrano-	Diplo-	Giganoto-	Veloci-	Ptero-	Mega-

Suffix

-saurus	-raptor	-mimus	-pteryx	-gnathus	-dactyl

Species name

regina	horribilis	deus	dominus	rex	magister

THIS DELIGHTFUL DINOSAUR IS CALLED:

....

Alien Artistry

Which body?

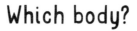

 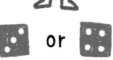 

or   or   or

Which eye(s)?

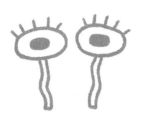    

Which mouth?

Draw your awesome alien in the frame.

DESIGN A DELICIOUS MEAL

This scrumptious meal is split into four equal parts.
You can draw each part in the space provided on your
plate. Roll a dice to create the best dinner in the world.

Roll 1:

Roll 2:

Roll 3:

Roll 4:

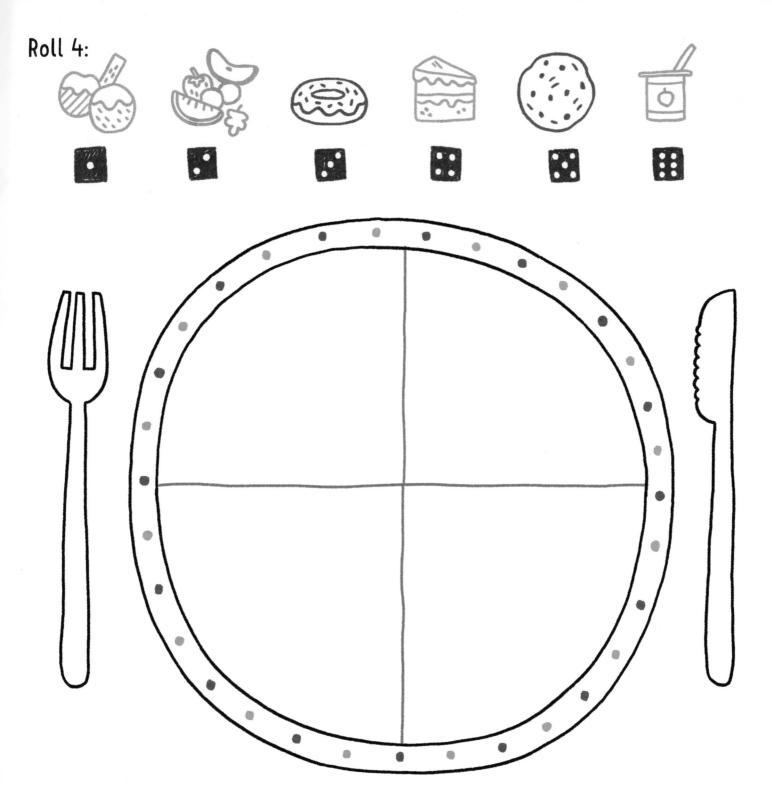

DESIGN A DISGUSTING DISH

Eurghhh! Gross! Design a disgusting dinner by rolling a dice in each round. This revolting meal is split into four equal parts. You can draw each part in the space provided on your plate.

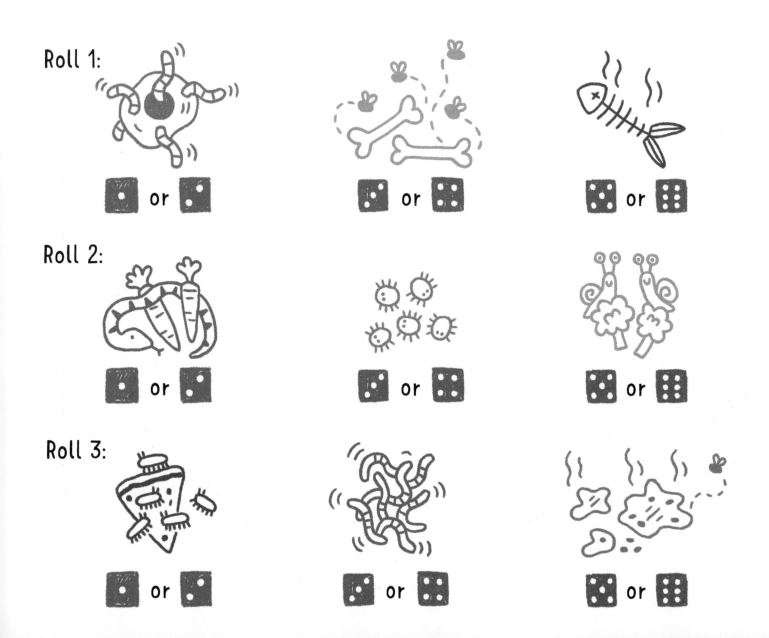

Roll 4:

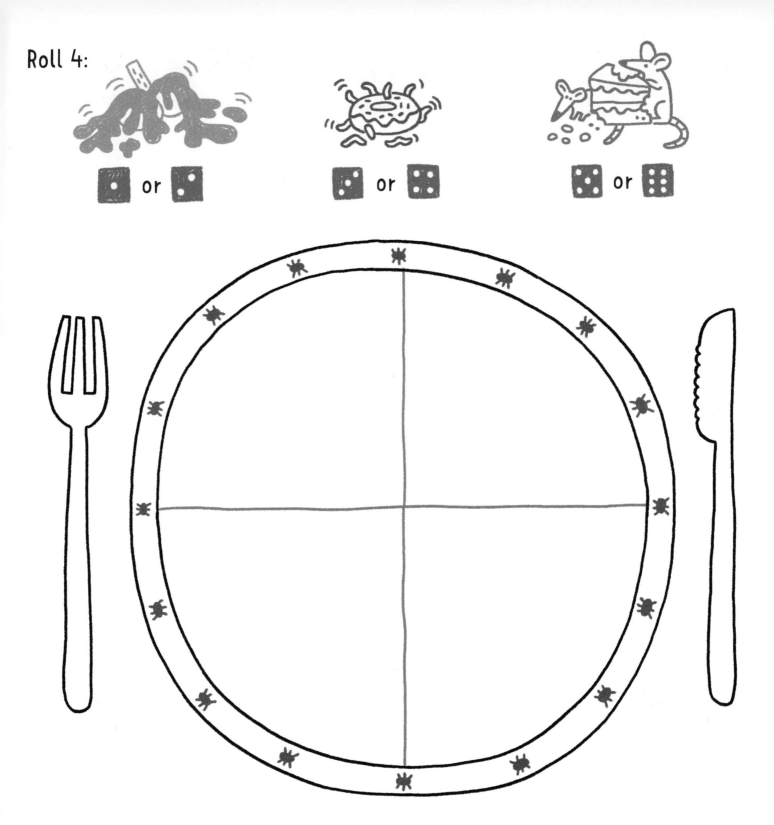

THE DOG DESIGNER

What breed is your dog?

 or   or   or

Which tail?

Which treat?

DRAW YOUR DOG IN THE FRAME.

The Cat Creator

Which head?

Which body?

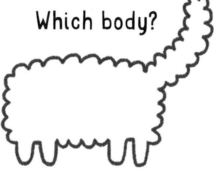

 or 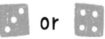   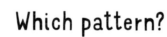 or   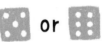 or

Which pattern?

Draw your cat in the frame.

NEW YEAR'S RESOLUTION

I PROMISE TO:

Help around the house

Draw more pictures

Learn magic

Read more

Play more sport

Learn to play an instrument

TRUTH OR DARE?

T: WHAT IS YOUR WORST HABIT?

D: TELL A JOKE TO THE FIRST PERSON YOU SEE

T: WHAT IS THE GROSSEST THING YOU'VE EVER DONE?

D: PRETEND TO BE A DINOSAUR FOR FIVE MINUTES

T: WHAT'S YOUR BIGGEST FEAR?

D: PUT YOUR CLOTHES ON BACK TO FRONT

Make A Misfit

Which head?

Which body?

Which legs?

Draw your marvellous misfit in the frame.

THE SHORT-STORY FACTORY:
Undead Aztec Adventure

NOUNS	ADJECTIVES	VERBS	RANDOM
ZOMBIE	SNOTTY	JUMP	EAR
MONKEY	LOST	RUN	LEG
SCIENTIST	STUPID	SCREAM	NOSE
BOTANIST	SLIMY	FART	HAND
ZOO KEEPER	GOOFY	DANCE	EYEBALL
TIGER	SHINY	SPIT	TONGUE

Roll a dice to complete the story on the opposite page. Each time you reach a dotted line, roll to select a random word from the column with the matching symbol.

Do not use the same word twice – roll until you get a new word.

I've been searching for the ☆☆☆☆☆☆☆☆☆☆☆☆☆☆☆☆☆☆☆☆☆☆☆
Chalice of the Undead King in the Amazon Rainforest.
I've befriended a faithful ⚭⚭⚭⚭⚭⚭⚭⚭⚭⚭⚭⚭⚭⚭⚭⚭⚭
to help me on my adventure.

We were deep in the jungle when my companion
decided to ＿＿＿＿＿＿＿＿＿＿＿＿. He'd found a stray
•••••••••••••••••••••• on the floor that must've belonged
to some sort of ⚭⚭⚭⚭⚭⚭⚭⚭⚭⚭⚭. On the ground,
next to the body part, was the chalice. I put it
in my rucksack and scratched my ••••••••••••••••••••••••.

I never saw the Undead King on my adventure,
but my travelling companion has long since
disappeared. A ☆☆☆☆☆☆☆☆☆☆☆☆☆☆☆☆ ••••••••••••••••••••••••••
is the only trace of him left.

            THE END

CREATE A CASTLE

Which style?

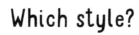

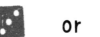 or

 or   or   or

Which flag?

Which portcullis/door?

DRAW YOUR CASTLE IN THE FRAME.

DOODLE A DRAGON

Which head?

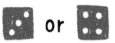

Which body?

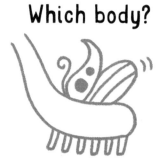

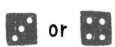

Which tail?

What will it breathe?

DRAW YOUR DRAGON IN THE FRAME.

Design Your Own Spaceship

Which cone?

Which fuselage?

     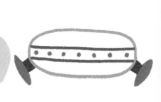

Which engines and flames?

Draw your spaceship
in this scene.

FATE AND FORTUNE

WHEN I GROW UP, I WILL BE A ...

 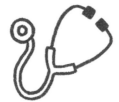    

VET	DOCTOR	LAWYER	WRITER	MUSICIAN	CHEF

I WILL LIVE IN A ...

HOUSE	FLAT	COTTAGE	CASTLE	MANSION	TREEHOUSE

I WILL TRAVEL AROUND USING MY ...

| TIME MACHINE | HORSE | MOTORBIKE | BROOMSTICK | BICYCLE | CAR |

....

I WILL HAVE A PET ...

RAT   DOG   CHAMELEON   TARANTULA   UNICORN   CAT

....

I WILL BE THE FIRST PERSON TO ...

WALK ON MARS

SOLVE WORLD POVERTY AND HUNGER

TRAVEL THROUGH TIME

BRING THE DINOSAURS BACK FROM EXTINCTION

COMMUNICATE WITH ANIMALS

DISCOVER ALIENS

....

....

ASK ME ANYTHING

Use your dice as a fortune teller by asking it random 'yes'/'no' questions. Each roll generates a reply from the options below. You could ask your dice if your secret crush likes you back, for example, or if you're having pizza for dinner!

 No way

 Probably

 No, not in a million years

 Yes, yes, yes!

 Ask me later

 Never ask again

SHADE IN SOME SUPERVILLAINS

What colour are their tops and leggings?
Roll once for each character.

Give each supervillain an emblem or crest.
Draw it in the empty space on each costume.

What colour are their boots and pants?
Roll once for each character.

What colour are their capes? Roll once for each character.

NAME YOUR SUPERVILLAINS

Roll once for each first name.

Doctor   Hunter   Acid   Wicked   Atomic   Omega

Roll once for each surname.

Nemesis   Nitro   Doom   Zero   Oddball   Strange

What powers will they possess?

The ability to bend metal   The ability to spit poison   The ability to shapeshift

The ability to bite ice cream   The ability to melt butter   The ability to vomit on command

MY NAME IS

....

SUPER POWER:

....

....

MY NAME IS

....

SUPER POWER:

....

....

MAKE SOME MODERN ART

Use different combinations to create your own gallery wall.

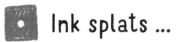 Ink splats ...

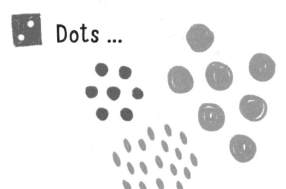 Dots ...

 Spirals ...

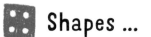 Shapes ...

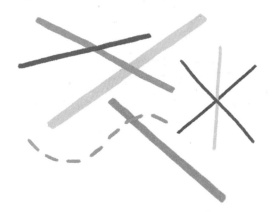 Lines ...

Squiggles ...

Don't forget to write your signature in a corner of each artwork.

Produce The Perfect Pet

Which head?

Which body?

Which legs?

Draw your perfect pet in the frame.

MAKE YOUR OWN MYTHICAL BEAST

Which head?

Which body?

Which legs?

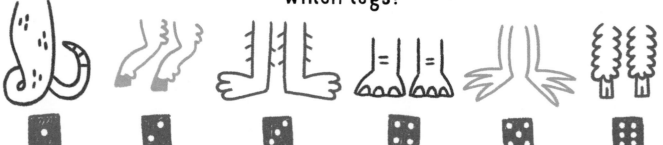

DRAW YOUR BEAST IN THE FRAME.

DOODLE BUG BINGO

Challenge a friend to see who can doodle a bug in the fastest time. You will need one dice each.

⚀	BODY	
⚁	HEAD	
⚂	LEGS	
⚃	EYES	
⚄	ANTENNAE	
⚅	SPOTS	

Each player MUST roll a '1' to begin. Once the body has been drawn, players MUST roll a '2'. From then on, any number can be rolled and the features added. The first player to finish WINS!

Doodle and draw your bugs on this page.

Create Some Cars

Which front?

Which middle?

    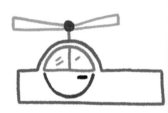

Which back?

Create one car in each frame above.

TRUTH OR DARE?

T: WHAT IS YOUR MOST EMBARRASSING MOMENT?

D: MAKE UP A FREESTYLE RAP

T: WHAT IS THE WEIRDEST THING YOU'VE EVER DONE?

D: ACT LIKE AN ANIMAL OF YOUR CHOICE FOR FIVE MINUTES

T: WHAT'S YOUR BIGGEST SECRET?

D: TALK IN A HIGH-PITCHED VOICE FOR THE NEXT FIVE MINUTES

Build Your Own Dice Decider

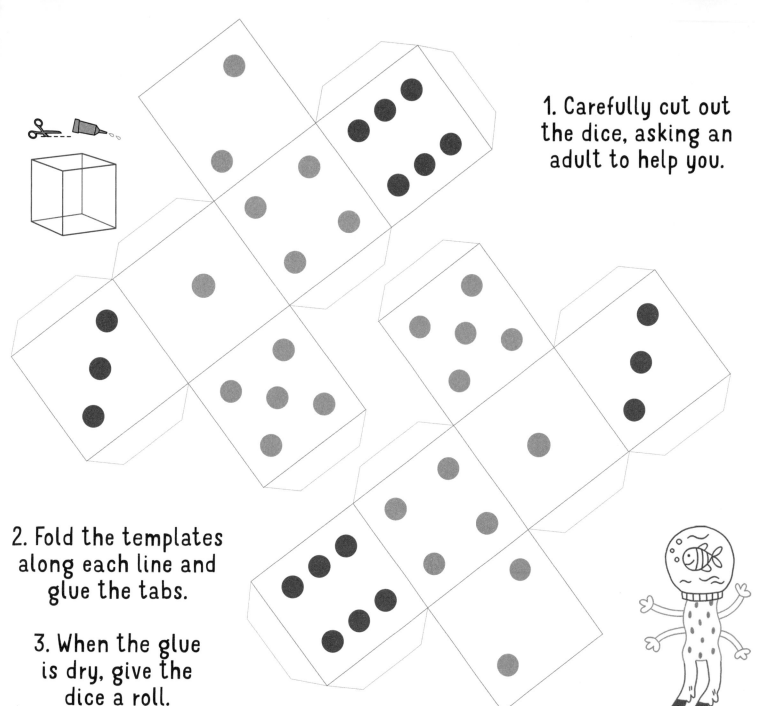

1. Carefully cut out the dice, asking an adult to help you.

2. Fold the templates along each line and glue the tabs.

3. When the glue is dry, give the dice a roll.

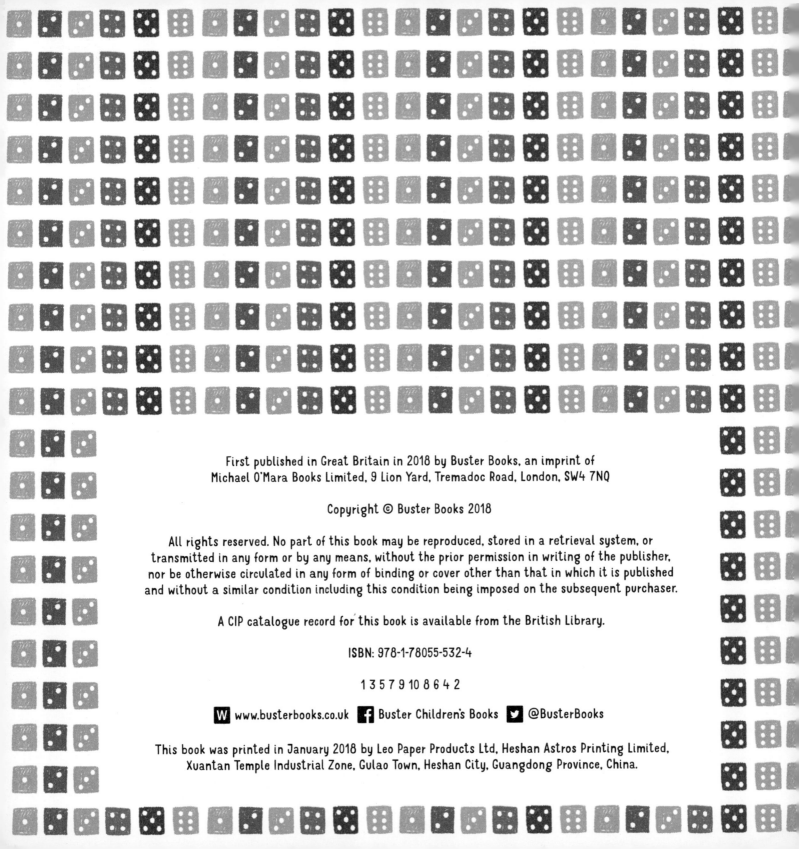

First published in Great Britain in 2018 by Buster Books, an imprint of
Michael O'Mara Books Limited, 9 Lion Yard, Tremadoc Road, London, SW4 7NQ

A CIP catalogue record for this book is available from the British Library.

ISBN: 978-1-78055-532-4

1 3 5 7 9 10 8 6 4 2

W www.busterbooks.co.uk   f Buster Children's Books   🐦 @BusterBooks

This book was printed in January 2018 by Leo Paper Products Ltd, Heshan Astros Printing Limited,
Xuantan Temple Industrial Zone, Gulao Town, Heshan City, Guangdong Province, China.